KU-224-444

CARDIFF MOBILE
☎ : 029 2076 3849

-3 MAY 2018
29 MAY 2018
14 JUN 2018

SAZ   BAT   SAZAKLIS, J.

The Battle of Optimus Prime

ACC. No: 05079951

ORCHARD BOOKS
Carmelite House
50 Victoria Embankment
London EC4Y 0DZ

First published as THE TRIALS OF OPTIMUS PRIME in 2016 in the United
States by Little, Brown and Company

This edition published by Orchard Books in 2017

HASBRO and its logo, TRANSFORMERS, TRANSFORMERS ROBOTS IN
DISGUISE, the logo and all related characters are trademarks of Hasbro
and are used with permission. © 2016 Hasbro. All Rights Reserved.

A CIP catalogue record for this book is available
from the British Library.

ISBN 978 1 40834 494 1

1 3 5 7 9 10 8 6 4 2

Printed and bound by CPI Group (UK) Ltd, Croydon, CR0 4YY

Orchard Books
An imprint of Hachette Children's Group
Part of The Watts Publishing Group Limited
An Hachette UK Company
www.hachette.co.uk

MIX
Paper from
responsible sources
FSC® C104740

The paper and board used in this book are made from wood from
responsible sources.

THE BATTLE OF OPTIMUS PRIME

BY JOHN SAZAKLIS

ORCHARD

MEET THE TEAM:

Bumblebee

Sideswipe

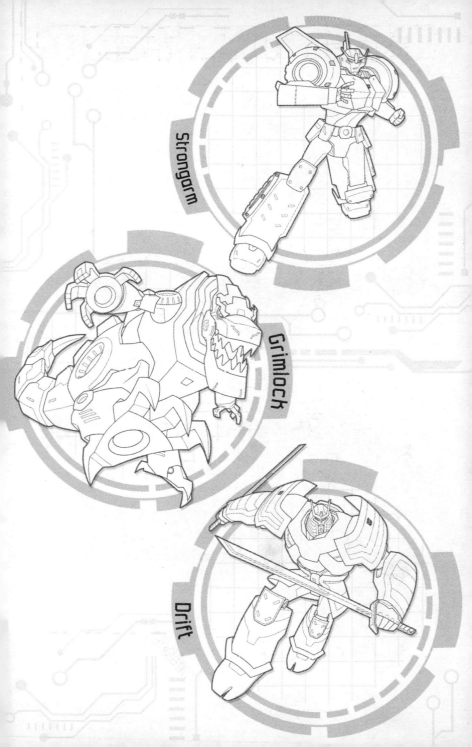

Strongarm

Grimlock

Drift

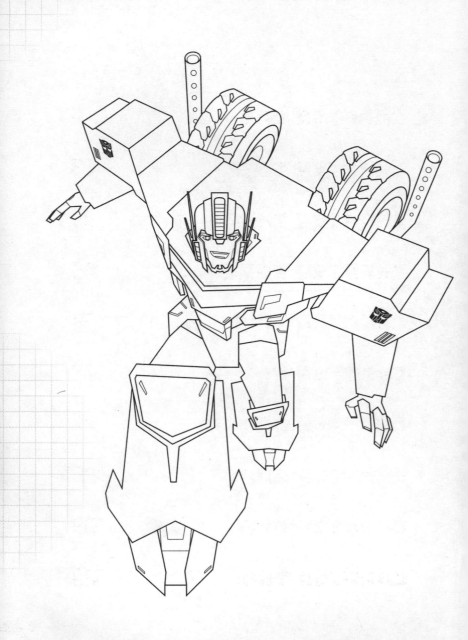

CONTENTS

STATUS REPORT: A prison ship from the planet Cybertron has crashed on Earth, and deadly robot criminals — the Decepticons — have escaped.

It's up to a team of Autobots to find them and get them back into stasis. Lieutenant Bumblebee, rebellious Sideswipe and police trainee Strongarm have taken the Groundbridge from Cybertron to Earth to track them down.

Along with bounty hunter, Drift, reformed Decepticon, Grimlock, and the malfunctioning pilot of the ship, Fixit, as well as the two humans who own the scrapyard where the ship crashed, Russell Clay and his dad, Denny, the robots in disguise must find the Decepticons, before they destroy the entire world ...

CHAPTER ONE

A MASSIVE RED-AND-BLUE TRUCK barrelled through a narrow canyon, sounding its booming horn.

Three other vehicles raced close behind it: a blue and white police car, a sleek red sports car, and a yellow sports car with black stripes.

At the opposite end of the canyon, an army of imposing figures stood armed and ready to fight. The truck and its convoy spat clouds of dust into the air as their spinning wheels tore across the sandy ground.

Moments before the truck collided with the edge of the army, its wheels left the ground, its shape twisted and changed in the air, and it revealed itself to be much more than just a vehicle – it was actually a robot in disguise!

"Autobots, attack!" the robot shouted, landing so one massive foot crushed an enemy to the ground.

The three other vehicles followed suit, lifting into the air and changing into robot modes of their own!

The army was composed of snarling, angular robots of a much more sinister variety: Decepticons. These terrible foes brandished wicked blades and maces.

The four Autobots stood together as a team, pushing back their attackers and knocking them off one by one with energy blasters and swords. The red-and-blue leader called the shots and looked out for his team-mates.

"Bumblebee, on your left!" the leader warned, directing the yellow-and-black bot to block an incoming blow.

CRASH!

The Decepticon staggered back and took out a few others as it fell.

"Sideswipe, take out that cannon!" the leader ordered.

The nimble red bot catapulted over a pile of rocks and sliced through a pair of Decepticons who were readying a massive energy cannon.

THUD!

The cannon hit the floor and blasted back a whole fleet of Decepticons.

CHOOM!

"Strongarm, create a perimeter for us!" Sideswipe shouted.

VROOM! The broad-shouldered blue bot changed back into her vehicle mode and plowed through the Decepticons, clearing a space for the Autobots to make a unified stand.

The enemies continued to swarm, but the four Autobots worked together like one well-oiled machine.

"Good job, Autobots! But this Decepticon horde doesn't seem to be getting any smaller. We need back up."

With a flick of his wrist, the Autobot leader summoned an energy shield to hold off the aggressive attackers. He spoke into the communicator embedded in his other arm.

"Fixit, we could use some extra feet on the ground right about now!"

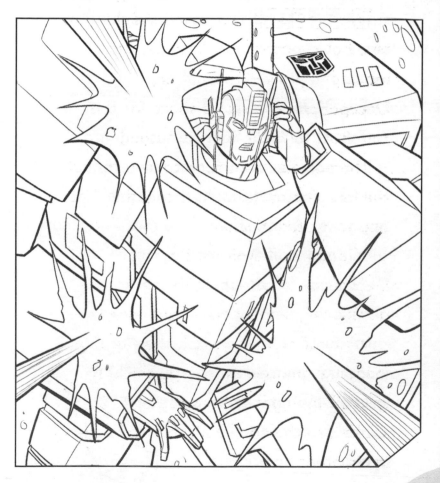

The communicator crackled and hissed.

As if on cue, a shape darkened the sky above the Decepticon army. Its shadow grew as it plummeted towards the ground.

BOOOOOM!

The formidable figure smashed into the gathered Decepticons, flattening the unlucky enemies caught beneath it. The impact emitted a shockwave that knocked many more off their feet.

"Thanks for dropping in, Grimlock," the leader quipped.

A huge black-and-green Dinobot climbed out of the crater that he had just

made, grinned, and joined the rumble.

"Any time!" he replied, stampeding through the horde.

The leader couldn't help smiling too.

Even as the enemy army doubled, then tripled, in size he was confident that his team could stand strong against the forces of evil. He continued to bark orders and provide covering fire while countless Decepticons poured down into the canyon.

Then, out of nowhere, a large swell of new enemies separated the huddled Autobots. The leader couldn't watch his team-mates' backs any more. He heard a pained cry ring out – and then it was cut short.

"Sideswipe!"

The red bot had fallen and was quickly covered by Decepticons.

Then another scream echoed through the canyon.

"Strongarm, no!" Optimus cried.

The blue police-bot dropped against the canyon wall and was similarly overtaken.

The leader's resolve began to crack, and the confidence he felt moments ago left him. He searched through the crowd for his remaining team-mates. It wasn't not too late to rally and force the Decepticons back ...

A deep groan and an earthshaking thud told him that the large Dinobot had been defeated, too. Beating back Decepticons on every side, the leader pushed through to the yellow-and-black bot's position. Blades sliced and maces smashed against his plating as he prioritised the search for his last standing team-mate over his own safety.

Cannons fired around him into the canyon walls, throwing dust and rock shards into the air. Optimus heard a familiar cry and saw a blur of yellow fall towards the ground.

"Bumblebee!" the leader shouted. With a wide swoop of his sword, he knocked back a swarm of enemies to reveal the crumpled shape of the last remaining member of his team.

"No, not you, too," he whispered, kneeling beside his friend. The yellow-and-black bot barely moved.

"Optimus …" Bumblebee struggled to speak. All the leader could do was look down at his injured comrade.

"Optimus …" Bumblebee gasped.

The dazed Decepticons picked themselves up and surrounded the duo. Escape was impossible.

The Autobot leader, Optimus, was soon covered on all sides, stumbling under the combined weight of his faceless assailants.

He struggled and strained to hear what Bumblebee was trying to tell him over the din of the Decepticon army.

And suddenly, it was clear what
Bumblebee was saying: "Optimus ... you
failed us!"

CHAPTER TWO

FOR A FEW NANOCYCLES, everything was dark. Then, one by one, the Decepticons who were piled on top of Optimus blinked out of existence, like the static hum of a television set.

The defeated Autobots were the only ones left in the canyon.

Optimus eyed the broken frames of his team-mates, until those, too, faded away.

The leader looked down into his arms just in time to catch the last hazy shadow of Bumblebee, before he too disappeared from sight.

"Not as ready as you thought you were, are you, hotshot?" The voice rang out from the canyon walls above.

The next time it spoke, it came from a different direction. "I hate to be so hard on you, but taking it easy never helped anyone."

Optimus squinted up into the harsh light, looking for the source of the voice.

"Down here, big guy," the voice said, suddenly appearing behind the Autobot.

It was a short green bot with bulky shoulders and a wide, square jaw. He hovered cross-legged a few feet off the canyon floor.

As he spoke, the canyon walls started to dissolve in a flurry of light, until the space around the two bots became a vast, nondescript void.

"My team ..." Optimus mumbled, as if

he was waking up from a dream.

"They weren't your *real* team-mates, Optimus, just holograms of the bots down on Earth," the floating figure replied. "And you barely know them. Except for that yellow one, I guess. And maybe I went too far by giving it dialogue processors."

Optimus narrowed his optics.

"Those bots are Bumblebee's team-mates. That makes them my allies, too. And I couldn't save them."

The green bot chuckled.

"Well, this time they were only holograms. Just like all the Decepticons who whooped your rear bumper. Not that it makes your new dents and scratches feel any better, I'm sure."

Optimus surveyed the damage from the simulated battle.

Despite the seemingly sharp weapons of the holographic Decepticons, his wounds were no more than surface-deep. The simulation wasn't meant to actually harm him, only to test him.

The other bot waved his hand and a shimmering light passed over Optimus, fixing the damage.

"Thank you, Micronus," Optimus said, bowing his head in respect. "The Realm of the Primes is still so disorienting to me. I know I am here to train and prepare myself for the battle ahead, but these simulations feel so real ..."

"Would they do you any good if they didn't?" Micronus shot back.

Micronus was one of the Thirteen, the
original Transformers created by Primus
to battle Unicron eons ago. Each was
designated a Prime and given
unique powers and
abilities.

Micronus was
the very first
Mini-Con, a
race of small
Cybertronians
with the ability to
enhance the powers
of their allies.

Ever since Optimus Prime had made the
ultimate sacrifice to restore the AllSpark
to their home planet of Cybertron, he
had existed in the Realm of the Primes.

Here, he had been strengthening himself physically and mentally for an unknown battle to come. Micronus had been serving as his teacher ... and he hadn't been easy on his pupil.

"Now shake it off. We're far from done here," Micronus said.

"I need to return to Earth," Optimus replied. "Every day that passes is another day that the Decepticons could strike. I have to get back. Bumblebee and the others need me."

Micronus scrutinised his student.

"Do they need you ... or is it that you need them?"

Optimus didn't respond.

"The city of Pellechrome wasn't built in a millennium," Micronus said. "And you

just completely scrapped your training.
I'm not exactly shooting confidence in your
abilities out of my tailpipe right now."

"I understand your reservations,
Micronus," Optimus replied. "But I've faced
Megatron. I've stood against Unicron. And
now it's time for me to rejoin my team
down on Earth."

"You're serious, aren't you?" Micronus
asked with a scoff. "All right, I'll convene
with the other Primes to discuss this. No
promises, though. You're still rough around
the grill as far as I'm concerned."

Before Optimus could thank the elder
bot, Micronus faded away in a glimmer of
sparks, leaving Optimus alone in the Realm
of the Primes.

An unknown distance away, Micronus reappeared, hovering in the shadow of a council of immense bots: the Primes. Of these powerful beings, only Micronus had chosen to reveal himself to Optimus.

"OK, fellas," Micronus said, comfortable amongst his brethren. "The kid is getting antsy. He wants to return to Earth."

A booming laugh broke out amongst the shadowed Primes.

"He's bold enough to suggest that he is ready after failing against a mob of your conjured Decepticons?" a deep voice asked, sounding surprised.

"Is he bold or is he stupid?" a cackling voice chimed in.

Micronus turned towards its source.

"Optimus is far from stupid, Liege Maximo," he retorted. "When he's ready, he will be one of our best chances at beating back the growing darkness. Not that I would expect you to care about saving the universe."

The figure with the deep voice spoke again to Micronus.

"You are right to believe in Optimus's potential, but he is not yet ready. We have been too easy on him, and his progress has faltered as a result. We charge you, Micronus, with making his training more rigorous. When he does return to Earth, he must be prepared."

"Your wish is my command sequence, brothers," Micronus replied, fading away to give Optimus the disappointing news.

As the other Primes drifted off, Liege Maximo remained. He pulled his cape around his frame and flexed the imposing horns on his head.

"Perhaps *I* should care more about Optimus's training ..." Liege Maximo said aloud to himself, forming a plan. "After all, having a new plaything might help relieve my boredom!"

CHAPTER THREE

"WELL, DON'T ACT SURPRISED,"
Micronus told Optimus as the Autobot
leader processed his disappointment.
"We didn't bring you here for scraps and
giggles, we brought you here to prepare
to face unimaginable evil."

"Worse than Unicron and Megatron?"
Optimus asked. "Because I defeated them
– with my team. I trust Bumblebee to
protect Earth in my absence, but what if
this great evil strikes before the Primes
think I'm ready?"

Micronus hovered high above Optimus.
He waved his hands and four enormous
bots suddenly rose out of the ground.

Each was outfitted with hefty shoulder cannons – pointed straight at Optimus!

"You think you're ready? Prove it."

Optimus flexed his pistons.

"Bring it on!" he shouted.

"Oh, we're going to make things a little more interesting now," Micronus responded.

He let out a laugh and waved his hand.

Glimmering buildings rose out of the ground, creating an approximation of a city on Earth. With another wave of his hand, smaller holograms of humans appeared.

"Think you can keep these ones safe?" As soon as Micronus issued his challenge, the four weaponised bots split up and darted after different groups of the holographic civilians.

Optimus sprang into action!

He chased after the biggest bot and leaped onto its back. Then he unsheathed his energy sword and wedged it under the bot's shoulder cannon.

SHTICK!

The bot tried to shake Optimus loose, but Optimus used all of his weight to pry the cannon free from its shoulder mount.

With a leap backwards, Optimus landed with the cannon in one arm and holstered his sword.

Then Optimus tugged on the cannon's firing mechanism, blasting the big bot off its feet in a noisy explosion of energy.

CHOOM!

"One down, three to go!"

With one group of civilians safe, Optimus hoisted the cannon onto his shoulder and aimed it towards another adversary.

BOOM!

Optimus dropped the cannon and darted after the remaining robots.

"Don't get cocky, Optimus!" Micronus shouted.

"Oh no, please *do* get cocky, Autobot," another voice whispered, just out of audio receptor distance. "And reckless. It will be much more fun if you're reckless!"

Micronus and Optimus didn't know it, but they had an unseen guest watching them: Liege Maximo!

Liege Maximo was not evil, but his petty jealousy and boredom made him a tricky troublemaker.

While Optimus chased down the third bot, Liege Maximo pulled the fourth one into an alley. He twitched his horns and reprogrammed the bot – making it bigger and stronger and much more vicious in its attacks! He also installed a few surprises for Optimus.

His meddling accomplished, Liege Maximo slipped away out of sight. He settled into a spot high up on one of the fake buildings where he could watch all the chaos.

Just then, Optimus subdued the third bot, saving the humans from being harmed.

"Last one, Optimus! It's closing time!"

Micronus called.

The brave Autobot leader dashed through the holographic streets, eager to find his final foe.

But before he could, a cannon blast knocked him off his feet and sent him flying into a nearby wall.

CRASH!

"Ouch! These simulations aren't playing around!"

Optimus climbed to his feet and rushed towards the source of the blast.

When the bot charged up for a second cannon blast, Optimus summoned his energy shield.

The bot fired, but Optimus deflected the blast.

FWOOM!

The Autobot leader drew his sword and watched his attacker's arms suddenly turn into spinning saw blades!

"Saving the worst for last, Micronus?" Optimus asked under his breath.

But Micronus was puzzled by this development.

"I may be many eons old," he said to himself, "but I'm pretty sure I didn't summon attack-bots with saw-blade arms ..."

Meanwhile, Optimus pedalled backwards, stepping out of the path of the spinning blades.

The attack-bot pressed forward, preparing to fire its cannon again!

Optimus pulled up his shield, just as a large volley of energy – much larger than before – shot directly at him.

His shield splintered, but not before reflecting the bulk of the blast, aiming it back at the bad bot.

KABOOM!

When the dust cleared, Optimus found himself in the wreckage of one of the holographic buildings. He stumbled into the street and saw what was left of his opponent: a lone saw blade rolling across the pavement.

Optimus hadn't survived unscathed, though. His injuries felt much more serious than before, as if this simulation was actually meant to hurt him!

Luckily, none of the simulated humans had been in this part of the city. Despite the damage he'd sustained, Optimus felt

Micronus's training exercise with Optimus – and getting away with it. He summoned a crude version of the Autobot leader. He threw his cape over his shoulder and began to slowly pace away from the motionless mannequin.

"Optimus, Optimus, Optimus … so eager to prove yourself that you'll suffer through pain," Liege Maximo said aloud.

As he paced, he pulled a small handful of dangerously sharp darts out of a holster near his waist. "I suppose the one question left to answer …"

Liege Maximo spun on his heels and

quickly threw the sharp metal darts. They embedded themselves in the fake Optimus's head. " … is just how much pain can you take?"

CHAPTER FOUR

MICRONUS LED OPTIMUS THROUGH the Realm of the Primes. Although he didn't mention it, Micronus noticed that the Autobot leader was walking with a slight limp.

"It's not time for you to return to Earth, Optimus," Micronus said. "But that doesn't mean you can't check in on things down there."

Micronus stopped at the base of a hill. He waved his hands in a familiar gesture and then urged Optimus to climb the hill. The Autobot leader did as he was instructed and found a reflecting pool at the top. Through it, he could see Earth!

"I think you've earned a break," Micronus said, turning to give Optimus some privacy. "Consider it a reminder of what you're fighting for."

The Prime disappeared, leaving Optimus alone with the portal.

As Optimus peered into it, his friends began to come into view ...

"Go long, Sideswipe!" Rusty Clay shouted, running backwards and winding his arm up to throw a rugby ball.

"Let it rip, Rusty!" Sideswipe hollered, nimbly running through the junk-filled aisles of the scrapyard.

Rusty was the son of Denny Clay, owner of the scrapyard that Bumblebee and his team of Autobots had been calling home while they were on Earth.

Sideswipe had been a bit of a rebel back on Cybertron, but even though he had a bit of an authority problem, he was now an invaluable member of the Autobot team.

Rusty let the ball fly through the air. It flew through the sky in a perfect arc … until a pair of giant metal jaws chomped down on it, instantly deflating it!

"HOLE IN ONE!" Grimlock shouted, the now-useless rubber of the ball dangling from his open mouth.

Grimlock was a reformed Decepticon. What he lacked in common sense, he made up for in strength, loyalty, and enthusiasm.

"Yeah, hole in one, all right – a hole in the *one* lob-ball we had!" Sideswipe said, yanking the remains out from Grimlock's teeth.

"That was a rugby ball, not a lob-ball, Sideswipe," Rusty said with a frown. "And 'hole in one' is from a different sport …"

"Don't feel bad, Russell Clay," Fixit said, patting Rusty on the back. "I can fit … flip … fix it right up!"

Sideswipe handed the deflated ball to Fixit, the team's Mini-Con.

Fixit was the pilot of the Alchemor, the maximum-security prison transport ship that crashed on Earth, releasing Decepticon prisoners across the planet.

The crash also damaged Fixit's speech modules, which is why he sometimes trimmed ... tricked ... tripped over his words!

"That's OK, Fixit. I'm sure my dad has some 'vintage' footballs around here somewhere," Rusty said.

"Nonsense! I'll repair this in two nano-cycles," Fixit said. The little Mini-Con shifted his hand into a complex drill tool.

Before Rusty could stop him, Fixit had somehow made the ball even worse.

"Oh my! This doesn't seem to have worked at all!" he said, sounding surprised.

Across the scrapyard, Bumblebee sat at the command centre computers with Strongarm, his eager, law-abiding second-in-command. While the others played, Bumblebee and Strongarm used the computer's sensors to search for Decepticon fugitives roaming the area.

"Strongarm, why don't you go and join the other bots?" Bumblebee suggested to his lieutenant. "It looks like our Decepticon pals are lying low today. You should relax a little."

"No, thank you, sir," Strongarm replied, straightening into a salute. "My place is at your side."

"I think you should take your place a little less seriously once in a while, cadet."

Strongarm frowned.

"How about this: I order you to keep an eye on the others," Bumblebee said, approaching the request a different way.

"And if you happen to have fun, that's permissible."

Strongarm maintained a serious look on her face. "Sir, yes, sir!" she said, marching outside to join the others.

Bumblebee shook his head as the cadet left the command center.

"Was I ever that eager?" Bumblebee wondered aloud to himself.

Back in the Realm of the Primes, Optimus smiled down at his former lieutenant.

"You certainly were, Bumblebee."

"Why aren't you ever that excited to see me?" Micronus asked, suddenly appearing in front of Optimus. Micronus gestured at the portal and it began to close, cutting off Optimus's brief glance at his Autobot team-mates.

"Bumblebee has assembled a good team down there," Optimus said. "I don't know if he realises it yet, but he has."

As Optimus limped away from the hill, following the hovering form of Micronus, a third figure slinked up to where the portal just closed.

"You're going to be even more fun than I had hoped, Optimus!" Liege Maximo whispered, his horns twitching.

He waited for the two bots to clear the area and then repeated the gesture that Micronus had made. Immediately, the portal reopened, focusing back on Bumblebee, still sitting at the computer console.

"It's showtime!" Liege Maximo said, grinning menacingly.

CHAPTER FIVE

BUMBLEBEE TAPPED AT THE KEYS, HIS optics growing weary from staring at the facts and figures spread across multiple screens.

The other Autobots, now joined by Strongarm, were messing around elsewhere in the scrapyard.

The mysterious and stoic Autobot Drift, a recent ally, was off on his own scouting mission with his two Mini-Cons, Slipstream and Jetstorm.

Denny Clay was in the diner he called home, cataloguing barbarian toys from the eighties that he purchased online.

Bumblebee didn't know it, but the

scheming Liege Maximo was watching him from the Realm of the Primes, outside of normal space and time.

Liege Maximo delighted in causing disruption, and he now knew that Bumblebee and Optimus held a deep bond of respect for each other – which he could use to cause trouble!

Summoning his powers of manipulation, Liege Maximo created an image of Optimus on one of Bumblebee's screens. Bumblebee was so used to processing data that he didn't think much of it.

"When did I pull up this profile of Optimus?" Bumblebee asked out loud to himself.

He attempted to click it away, but he couldn't find a way to dismiss the file.

As his confusion mounted, a familiar voice echoed through the speakers.

"BUMBLEBEE!"

Bumblebee nearly toppled backwards!

Since Optimus had awoken in the Realm of the Primes, he had occasionally appeared to Bumblebee to deliver messages of encouragement or warnings against danger. But showing up on Bumblebee's computer was a first!

"Optimus? You startled me!" Bumblebee said, calming down. "What's the glitch? Do we need to prepare for an attack?"

"YES, BUMBLEBEE!" the voice boomed once more.

Bumblebee was nervous – this wasn't like the previous visions he'd received.

"YOU MUST PREPARE FOR A
TERRIBLE ATTACK!"

The yellow Autobot shouted into his
wrist communicator for his team to
assemble in the command centre
immediately. He turned back to the
screen.

"What kind of attack, Optimus? From
whom?"

"FROM ME!"

The image of Optimus began to laugh
terribly before turning to static. The
speakers fizzed and shot sparks across
the floor.

Bumblebee was stunned into silence.

Before he could process what just
happened, the rest of his team poured
into the command centre.

"What's wrong, sir?" Strongarm asked as she reached Bumblebee's side.

"I ... I saw ..." Bumblebee couldn't think of a way to explain what he'd just witnessed.

When he had first started seeing Optimus, his team-mates hadn't believed him. It wasn't until Optimus Prime had appeared in real life to help them out that everyone had accepted it.

There's no way they were going to believe that Optimus just showed up to warn Bumblebee that HE was going to attack!

"What did you see, Bee?" Sideswipe asked, impatient to know what was going on.

"I saw …" Optimus started.

"Skinkbomb!" Fixit shouted, pointing at the screen behind Bumblebee. "Our leader must have spotted Skinkbomb, the Decepticon demolitions expert. His radar blip just appeared on-screen!"

Fixit's treads rolled across the floor to the console. His digits tip-tapped across the keys and pulled up a profile for Skinkbomb. The Decepticon was broad and stocky, with reptilian features and a wide, squat tail.

Fixit chuckled to himself.

"No wonder Bumblebee is speechless – Skinkbomb has quite an ugly mug!"

"You got that right," Grimlock said with a grin. "And that tail don't look too pretty neither."

"Skinkbomb was apprehended for unauthorised demolitions on Cybertron," Fixit informed the group. "But he's explosive even without his bombs. His tail is actually a miniature warhead of its own, which he can detach at will and regrow by consuming metal and oil."

Strongarm looked expectantly at Bumblebee, who was still rattled by the sinister message from Optimus.

"Um, sir ..." Strongarm said, nudging Bumblebee discreetly.

The Autobot leader realised his team was staring at him.

"Oh, right," he mumbled. "Let's, um, get out there and ... arrest ... this Decepticon."

The other bots exchanged a look.

Their leader's attempt at trying to coin a catchphrase were always bad, but this one was especially pathetic.

"Wow," Sideswipe whispered to Grimlock. "Bee really dropped the lob-ball on that one, didn't he?"

Moments later, the Autobots were rolling out of the scrapyard.

According to Fixit's monitoring devices, Skinkbomb was at the base of the Crown City Bridge. Bumblebee and his team needed to move fast to prevent a catastrophe!

When they arrived, Strongarm, along with Denny and Rusty in police uniform disguises, headed for the bridge's

entrance to block the oncoming traffic
and clear the road of people.

Bumblebee led Sideswipe and Grimlock
under the bridge to confront Skinkbomb
at the water's edge.

Strongarm, in her police car vehicle
mode, used her megaphone to help
convince people of the urgency of the
evacuation above. Within a few minutes,
the bridge was cleared.

Rusty and Denny stayed at the
barriers while Strongarm headed to the
base of the bridge to join her team-mates
in a volatile battle.

KABOOM!

Skinkbomb was slow and bulky, but he
was handy with explosives. Each time the
Autobots got close, Skinkbomb hurled a

grenade to keep them at a distance.

"Boom! You get an explosive! You get an explosive!" Skinkbomb yelled, then vibrated with a deep, unhinged laugh. "I'll blow us all to bolts before I go back to the lockup!"

Skinkbomb chucked a bomb towards Bumblebee, who dived out of the way in time to miss most of the blast.

The Autobot landed in the water below the bridge. As he lifted himself out of the murk, a face slowly came into focus through the rippling water.

"BUMBLEBEE!"

Bumblebee rubbed his optics, convinced that it must be a trick of the water.

"I'VE SEEN THE ERROR OF MY WAYS, BUMBLEBEE," the vision of

Optimus said to his former protégé. "ALIGNING OURSELVES WITH THE WEAK AUTOBOTS WAS A MISTAKE," Optimus continued.

Bumblebee looked back at his team.

Grimlock, Sideswipe, and Strongarm were working together to get close enough to apprehend Skinkbomb, but the Decepticon was holding them off.

"What are you talking about, Optimus? You're a hero!"

"I WAS A FOOL!" the voice bellowed. "BUT NOW I AM STRONG."

Optimus's optics took on an eerie blue glow.

Bumblebee glanced at his team once more as they struggled against their powerful foe. In battle against a dangerous Decepticon like Skinkbomb, every nanocycle counted!

He wanted to go help them, but he was frozen in anticipation of what this vision of Optimus would say next.

"NOW," Optimus roared, "I AM A DECEPTICON!"

CHAPTER SIX

"WATCH OUT, BEE!" SIDESWIPE yelled. The Autobot leader was distracted by the vision of an evil Optimus.

The agile young bot tackled Bumblebee, pushing him out of the way of one of Skinkbomb's explosives.

BOOM!

Bumblebee was slammed into one of the bridge support pillars by the force of the blast. His audio receptors were ringing and his entire chassis was rattling. He felt bruised all over, but otherwise unharmed.

But what about his team-mate?

"Sideswipe!"

Bumblebee splashed through the shallow water to Sideswipe's side. The ninja-like Autobot was badly injured, having taken the brunt of the explosion while saving Bumblebee.

"Sideswipe, I need to get you out of here," Bumblebee said.

The battered bot struggled to speak.

"Don't sweat it, Bee ... just make sure you take out ... that Decepti ..." Sideswipe's voice trailed off.

Bumblebee propped Sideswipe up against a bridge support pillar and rushed back to the fight.

Grimlock and Strongarm were still dodging explosive blasts, seeking any opportunity to dash in and attack Skinkbomb.

When the dangerous Decepticon spotted a very angry and determined Bumblebee charging in his direction, he knew his luck was running out.

"Uh-oh, looks like it's time to bring the house down!"

The demolitions expert spun around and revealed his tail. It was glowing! Skinkbomb had set off his tail bomb!

With a grinding of gears, Skinkbomb's tail came loose.

"Hasta la vista, babies!" Skinkbomb shouted as he made a break for it. "Exit, stage left!"

Bumblebee ground to a halt a few feet from the tail.

Grimlock and Strongarm both raced after Skinkbomb, but Bumblebee yelled after them. "There's no time, Autobots! Find cover, now!"

The flashing light on the detached tail was glowing brighter and brighter.

The team ran towards the support pillars, Bumblebee carrying Sideswipe over his shoulder.

The four Autobots ducked behind the thick concrete just as—

BOOOOOOOOOM!

The force of the blast made the bridge groan and sway.

Luckily, Strongarm and Grimlock had led Skinkbomb far enough away that there was no structural damage to the bridge.

Unfortunately, the explosion had given the Decepticon plenty of time to escape,

and with an injured Autobot and no
arrest, the mission was officially a failure.

In the Realm of the Primes, Liege Maximo
cackled with delight. By briefly
pretending to be Optimus, he had sown
discord amongst all the Autobots on
Earth.

"They must think their fearless leader
has brain rust!"

Pleased with himself, Liege Maximo
closed the portal to Earth and travelled
through the Realm to check in on the
real Optimus and his training under
Micronus.

He found the pair meditating on top of
two towering pillars.

"This doesn't look challenging at all," Liege Maximo whispered.

He used his immense abilities to create a small fleet of sharp-limbed drone robots. Using their bladed arms, they quickly scurried up the pillars.

Without warning, the drones attacked Optimus!

Before the Autobot could react, several of their blades sliced against his frame, leaving painful rivets in the steel.

SLASH! SLASH!

"Micronus! Are you warning me never to let my guard down?" Optimus summoned his shield and unsheathed his sword.

The drones continued to swarm around him, their claws thrashing wildly.

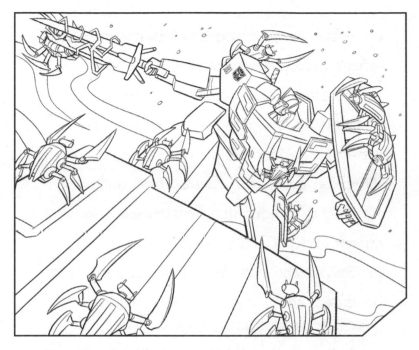

Optimus blocked the blows and attacked back when he could, careful to maintain his balance on the massive column.

Micronus was jarred out of his meditation by the clashing of blades. He looked across the divide between their pillars and found Optimus in battle

against a small army of bladed assailants
– bots he hadn't summoned!

The pint-sized Prime rose from his
position on the pillar. With one wave of
his hand, he lifted Optimus up into the air.
With another, he removed both pillars,
sending the sharp little attackers
plummeting. They smacked into the
ground, shattered into flecks of light, and
disappeared.

SKEESH!

Micronus lowered himself down and
brought Optimus with him.

"I don't understand," Optimus said. "Did
I perform the trial wrong?"

"No, Optimus," Micronus responded.
"You weren't wrong – the attackers were.
I didn't create those bots. Which means

that something is rotten in the Realm. Someone is interfering with your training."

Optimus looked around him for a likely culprit, but the Realm of the Primes is an immense, shadowy place with an ever-changing landscape. Anyone wishing to hide would have plenty of places to do so.

"I need to convene with the rest of the Primes and discuss this troubling development."

Micronus created a large, flat-topped pyramid out of the ground.

"You stay here. I don't want you caught by surprise until we find out who's behind all this."

Optimus climbed to the top of the pyramid, where he can see most of the land around him.

"Micronus, are the other Primes testing me, too?" he asked. "I ... I don't want to fail them."

"If they were, I'd know," Micronus replied. "And wrecking you here wouldn't do us any good back on Earth or Cybertron."

Micronus pointed to Optimus's very real dents and scratches when he said this.

The Prime disappeared, leaving Optimus alone.

Far in the distance, Liege Maximo grinned wickedly. Now Micronus was gone, his new plaything was all his!

Back on Earth, Strongarm and Grimlock helped Bumblebee load Sideswipe onto

Fixit's repair table. The brash young
Autobot was badly banged up and
was drifting in and out of
rest mode.

"I've got him from here,
Bee," the Mini-Con said
cheerfully. "Nothing some
elbow grease can't fix! And
some Energon infusions. And
an extensive diagnostic repair kit—"

"We get it, Fixit," Bumblebee
interrupted. "Just make sure he's OK,
all right? It's my fault he's injured. I was
distracted. Sideswipe saved me from
getting hurt by taking the blast himself."

Grimlock and Strongarm looked away.
They weren't used to their leader being
so upset.

"I want you two to stay by his side," Bumblebee told them. "I'm going to track down Skinkbomb's whereabouts so we can put that dangerous dynamite stick back on ice." The Autobot leader took another look at Sideswipe and walked out of the repair center.

"Grimlock, did you see what distracted Bee during the fight?" Strongarm asked.

"Uhh ... it kind of looked like he was staring at his own reflection," Grimlock replied. "I like to look at my handsome face, too, but there's a time and a place, ya know?"

Fixit was eavesdroping on Strongarm and Grimlock's conversation while he was working at repairing Sideswipe.

"Was Bumblebee acting dazed and

confused without rear ... fear ... I mean, clear reason?" he asked.

Strongarm and Grimlock considered for a second, then both said, "Yes."

"Have there been moments recently when Bee seemed to be distant and aloof, as if he were in his own world?" Fixit asked.

Strongarm and Grimlock thought about it again, remembering Bee's odd behaviour in the command center before the mission. They nodded.

"Ah, it's very simple, then," Fixit said. "Our leader must be suffering from brain rust!"

The Autobots looked at each other in dismay.

CHAPTER SEVEN

STRONGARM AND THE OTHER members of Bumblebee's team on Earth weren't the only bots feeling worried.

Back in the Realm of the Primes, Micronus was again consulting with his brothers about Optimus's training.

"You told me to take it harder on the kid, not turn him into spare parts," Micronus said, hovering in front of the shadowy figures of the Primes. "And if you trust me to train him, you should let me know if you're going to stick your sprockets into the proceedings."

Micronus couldn't help a note of wounded pride from entering his voice.

"Has there been ... an incident?" a deep voice asked.

Micronus looked at the Primes with mounting confusion.

"You mean to tell me you haven't been sending your own bots after Optimus?" the miniscule bot asked. "Real aggressive ones, loaded up with pointy blades?"

The gathered Primes looked at one another for answers, but none claimed responsibility.

"Wait a minute," Micronus said suddenly. "Where is he? Where is that no-good, horn-headed, backstabbing bag of rust?"

The Primes stepped out of the shadows, revealing one fewer figure than the last time Micronus met with them.

"Where is Liege Maximo?" Micronus demanded.

Back at the pyramid, Optimus took advantage of his solitude to try out his sword techniques. Time didn't pass the same in the Realm of the Primes as it does on Earth or Cybertron, and the Autobot leader found that he rarely needed to rest.

Optimus's desire for justice and peace had always been enough to drive him, but he did miss working alongside his team-mates.

Unfortunately, Liege Maximo had figured this out from watching Optimus, and he had hatched a diabolical idea.

With a stir of his horns and a wave of his hands, the manipulative mischief-maker conjured up an approximation of Bumblebee, visually identical to the Autobot stationed back on Earth, except with a pair of creepy red optics.

Liege Maximo imbued the false bot with a devilish mean streak and then directed it towards Optimus's pyramid!

His plan in motion and a smirk on his face, Liege Maximo gathered his cape and retreated to a safe viewing distance. He created a curtain of fog to hide his presence.

"And now it's time for the second act!" he said.

In between thrusts of his blade, Optimus picked up on a slight noise, like treads scraping against the mysterious bedrock of the Realm. The red-and-blue hero glanced around, noticing the gathered fog for the first time.

"You're not going to catch me off guard, Micronus!" Optimus shouted into the near-total silence. He swung around with his blade drawn ... and came face-to-face with Liege Maximo's cruel creation!

"Bumblebee?" he gasped. Optimus was shocked at first, but remembered Micronus's holograms of his team-mates during the canyon simulation. The Autobot leader was a fast learner and a quick thinker. A trick like this couldn't fool him for long!

"Did Micronus create you to test my emotions?" Optimus asked.

The fake Bumblebee rushed forward and grabbed Optimus by the shoulders.

"I'm real, Optimus!" Bumblebee said. "And I'm here because we failed! Earth is lost!"

The Autobot leader staggered back, stepping out of the fake Bumblebee's grasp.

His confidence that this wasn't the real Bumblebee was slightly shaken.

"We couldn't stop what was coming without your help. Now the others are gone, and I'm stuck here in this weird place with you," the fake friend explained.

Optimus hesitated, but stood firm that the feeling in his bolts was true. This wasn't Bumblebee … he hoped.

"I don't believe you," he said. "Tell me something that only Bumblebee would know, something that will prove to me that you're the bot I've trusted by my side in the past – and that what you're saying about Earth is true."

The imposter bot stared at Optimus. Some distance away, Liege Maximo fumed with fury.

"Scrap! Curse that Optimus and his resistance to my trickery. I'll just have to use a little force!"

The Prime upgraded his creation to unnerve Optimus even more.

"Come on, buddy, you know it's me, deep in your spark," Bumblebee said, shaking the bigger bot's frame. "It's me … your ol' pal BEE!"

The evil imposter leaped at Optimus, red optics glaring.

With the back of his sword, Optimus thumped the phony Bumblebee on the head.

BONK!

"Is that how you treat an old friend?" the dazed doppelgänger whined.

Optimus unleashed a powerful kick

that sent Bumblebee tumbling off the pyramid. He slid down the side like a skater grinding a pipe, shooting up sparks as he goes.

By the time he reached the bottom, the mock Bumblebee had faded away like the other constructs of the Realm.

The fog disappeared, too.

"Micronus!" Optimus yelled. "Micronus, what sort of test is this?"

"No test of mine, for Solus Prime's sake," Micronus said, suddenly appearing behind Optimus.

With an aggressive wave of his hand, the pyramid rapidly flattened.

"Optimus, we have a big problem," Micronus said grimly. "And his name is Liege Maximo."

Some distance away from Optimus and Micronus, Liege Maximo continued to seethe.

"That humourless, rust-headed reject is ruining everything!" he said to himself. "This realm is endlessly boring and the other Primes are no fun at all. Now the first new plaything to come along in eons is already growing wise to my tricks!"

The bot paced back and forth, considering his options.

In the midst of his stomping, Liege Maximo noticed that he was near a small hill. He climbed the gentle slope and stared down into the pool at the top of it, the perfect plan leaping instantly into his manipulative mind.

"Well if Optimus won't play along, I'll turn my attention back to these *other* new toys."

With a wave of his hand, the pool at his feet stirred and revealed a window to another place, far away from the Realm of the Primes: the scrapyard on Earth, with the real Bumblebee and the other bots!

CHAPTER EIGHT

BUMBLEBEE ENTERED THE command center cautiously, remembering his vision of an evil Optimus. He didn't want to believe that those glimpses of his former leader were real, but they certainly felt like they were ...

Even if the visions were just hallucinations brought on by stress and pressure, they had thrown Bumblebee off his game during the Autobots' battle with Skinkbomb. He took full responsibility for the injuries Sideswipe had sustained, and the only way to make it up to him was to track down the escaped Decepticon!

Bumblebee ran his digits over the keys of the computer console, bringing it to electronic life. He pulled up Fixit's tracking software and set the radius as wide as it would go.

The outskirts of Crown City, where the team had first fought Skinkbomb, were clear of Decepticon life-forms. The forest around the scrapyard was likewise deserted.

The quarry on the other side of the forest, however, showed one big red blip on the radar!

"Bingo!" Bumblebee shouted. "I'm taking you down personally, you overgrown lizardbot!"

But as Bumblebee watched, the red blip on the radar flickered in and out like a dying lightbulb.

The Autobot leaned in closer to examine the screen. The light flickered again, and then a second red light popped into existence a short distance from the first.

"A second Decepticon!" Bumblebee said. "Skinkbomb must have an ally!"

The two lights flickered and blinked in unison like a pair of eyes.

"Are they trying to disguise their signals?" Bumblebee said to himself. "I've got to get the others and track these two down before they disappear!"

Just then, a loud, familiar voice came through the speakers.

"WHY DO YOU FIGHT AGAINST US, BUMBLEBEE?" the voice asked.

Bumblebee recoiled from the screen.

An outline appeared around the two red lights, bringing Optimus's face into view. The red eyes made the electronic picture of Bumblebee's former leader look even more sinister.

"JOIN ME, BUMBLEBEE, AND RULE BY MY SIDE WHEN MY DECEPTICONS SQUASH YOUR PUNY AUTOBOTS."

"Stop this, whoever you are!" Bumblebee yelled back at the screen. "I know you're not really Optimus. You're just a Decepticon trick, and Team Bee's specialty is taking you down!"

"TELL THAT TO SIDESWIPE ... IF HE RECOVERS!"

Bumblebee pulled back his fist, ready destroy the console.

"Sir, stop!" Strongarm shouted, appearing in the doorway to the command centre. "What are you doing?"

The Autobot leader turned around and took in the concerned faces of his team.

Strongarm, Grimlock, Fixit, Rusty, and Denny all stood back, cautiously keeping their distance from him.

"Can't you see?" Bumblebee asked, pointing behind him. "Somebot infected our systems with an evil version of Optimus!"

The team-mates looked at one another, worried, then frowned at their leader.

Bee turned back to the console and saw that the screen was displaying a normal map, with only one bright red blip in the quarry. The flashing red eyes and clear outline of Optimus's face were nowhere to be found.

"It ... it was right there just before you came in," Bumblebee tried to explain.

"It was taunting me and threatening our team!"

Fixit whispered to Denny and Russell, and the two humans left the room, concerned looks on their faces.

"Bumblebee, perhaps you should let me tick ... tock ... take a look at your wiring," the Mini-Con said, rolling towards the confused yellow bot. "The negative effects of group management stress are not to be underestimated and can lead to—"

"Wait a minute," Bumblebee interrupted, taking a step back. "Do you all think I'm malfunctioning?"

Strongarm, Grimlock, and Fixit exchanged worried glances.

Grimlock took a careful step forwards, his bulky arms outstretched.

"Let's all calm down, Bee," the Dinobot said, inching towards his leader. "We're all friends here, right?"

Bumblebee shook his head vigorously, clearing his thoughts.

"Grim, stop it, I'm not going to do anything crazy," he said.

The Dinobot continued to move closer until Strongarm elbowed him.

"I know what I'm saying sounds unusual, but hear me out. Somebot has been sending me evil visions of Optimus trying to distract me." Bumblebee tried to explain.

"I believe you, sir, but a tune-up never hurt anybot!" Fixit added, approaching

Bumblebee with forced cheerfulness.

"Fixit," Bumblebee said. "I don't have brain rust. I admit I'm shaken up by what happened to Sideswipe, but someone is messing with us and I intend to put an end to it!"

The other Autobots in the room looked at one another with renewed confidence in their leader.

"But first we have a Decepticon that deserves some payback," Bumblebee said, pointing at the red blip on the screen. "And, as Sideswipe would say, 'What goes around, comes around!'"

CHAPTER NINE

FAR AWAY IN THE REALM OF THE Primes, a very disgruntled Liege Maximo stomped and kicked at the ground.

"These Autobots are NO FUN AT ALL!" he bellowed, blowing up several fake bots.

"All I ask for in this vast, endless existence is some semblance of joy, and these boring bots are intent on keeping that away from me with their 'teamwork' and 'justice' and 'loyalty'! I can taste the fuel coming back up my intake valve!"

Liege Maximo's horns twitched, and a full legion of mindless bots appeared before him, covered in all manner of slicing blades, blunt maces, and spiky armour.

"If all those awful Autobots want is a fight to destruction, then I'll give them the destruction they seek!"

"Who is Liege Maximo?" Optimus asked, his frame tensing.

"He's very old," Micronus explained. "Liege Maximo is one of us, an original Prime and member of the Thirteen. Long, long ago, Liege Maximo grew bored of our existence. He's never been truly evil, but his cruelty and manipulation are legendary. To relieve his boredom, Liege Maximo uses his power to pit brother against brother for his own amusement."

"Brother against brother?" Optimus asked. "Micronus, before you arrived, I was attacked by something that took the shape of my team-mate, Bumblebee from Earth. It spoke in Bumblebee's voice and looked just like him, but the things he said ..."

"That sounds like Liege Maximo's doing, all right," Micronus said. "He is one of the Primes, and we tolerate him,

but his lies and treacheries have cost us dearly in the past. Now it looks like he's trying to have some twisted 'fun' with you."

Optimus narrowed his optics and pounded his mighty metal fists together.

"If this is Liege Maximo's idea of fun, then it's time we twist it back at him," Optimus said with gusto.

Micronus laughed.

"Optimus, you're not ready for a Prime!" Micronus said. "You'll meet Liege Maximo in time, and he might even teach you a thing or two worth knowing, but this is one problem you can't fight."

The Autobot leader's tactical brain raced with ideas.

"The false Bumblebee's patience didn't last very long when I called its bluff," Optimus said. "It seems like Liege Maximo gets bored of his games as soon as they don't go his way. I think we can use that to our advantage."

Micronus smiled. Maybe Optimus *was*
ready for this battle, after all ...

Back on Earth, Bumblebee led Strongarm
and Grimlock towards Skinkbomb's signal
in the quarry. Fixit, Rusty, and Denny
had stayed back in the scrapyard to take
care of Sideswipe. Bumblebee and
Strongarm's wheels tore rivets into the
ground, and Grimlock's pounding feet
shook the trees around them.

"You know I have utmost faith in you,
sir," Strongarm said to Bumblebee. "But
even if you're not suffering from early
symptoms of brain rust, we're still one
Autobot short and we're going up against

a Decepticon that nearly turned us into spare parts last time we squared off against him."

"Fixit said Skinkbomb needs to consume large amounts of metal and flammable oils to regrow his tail-bomb. If we can catch up to him before he's eaten enough, we may have the upper hand," Bumblebee said. "And this time, I won't be so easily distracted."

The others nodded, then they shifted into a higher gear, spitting grass and dirt behind him as they went.

Finally, Bumblebee, Strongarm, and Grimlock arrived at the edge of the quarry. The Autobot leader whispered into his wrist communicator.

"We're about to enter the quarry, Fixit. If you have any luck getting in touch with Drift, give him our coordinates."

The bots scanned the rocky landscape for any sign of their explosive enemy. Suddenly, there was a loud crunching noise.

They followed the noise around a bend and spotted Skinkbomb, guzzling a barrel of oil!

"Autobots, it's time to ignite the dynamite!" Bumblebee yelled.

His lame attempt at a catchphrase caused his team-mates to roll their optics, but it did catch Skinkbomb's attention.

The three bots charged from their hiding spot.

Bumblebee and Strongarm, still in their vehicle modes, crashed into Skinkbomb, knocking him off balance and causing him to spill the oil in his claws.

Grimlock leaped into the air and came thundering down on the Decepticon, knocking the wind out of his pistons and pinning him to the ground.

"Why don't you try eating my Dino-Destructo Double Drop instead?" the towering Dinobot yelled.

"You really think you goody two-treads could take me out that easy?" Skinkbomb asked, struggling under Grimlock's bulk. "Don't you know who I am?"

The Decepticon used his pinned arm to tap at a button on his side.

A cascade of small spheres poured out of the containers around his waist – microbombs!

"Uh-oh," Grimlock said.

KABOOM-BOOM-BOOM!

A series of explosions rang out around Skinkbomb, the sound and vibrations echoing loudly through the quarry.

Grimlock was thrown backward, giving Skinkbomb enough time to pull himself up and race back to the oil drums. The Decepticon started drinking the oil again.

118

Through the haze of dust and smoke, Bumblebee saw that Skinkbomb's tail was nearly regrown. He had to reach the Decepticon before he could finish his meal!

The yellow Autobot leaped into his bot mode and pulled out his blaster.

Bumblebee let loose a series of shots that made holes in the oil container like swiss cheese.

"Looks like you've sprung a leak, lizardbot!" Bumblebee cried.

His drink gone, the aggravated Skinkbomb hurled the rapidly emptying drum at Bumblebee's head.

The Autobot leader ducked just a nanocycle too late and the oil barrel caught him on the top of his head.

The force of the impact knocked him off
his treads, and he landed facedown in a
pool of spilled oil.

Bumblebee quickly scrambled up,

but not before catching his reflection in the oil – and watching it quickly turn into the sinister, grinning face of Optimus Prime!

CHAPTER TEN

LIEGE MAXIMO LOOKED DOWN into the portal to Earth, crowing in delight as he summoned an evil Optimus vision to taunt Bumblebee during the battle.

"Oh, is the little Autobot distracted by his big, bad friend?"

But as Liege Maximo celebrated, Micronus suddenly appeared behind him.

"Sticking your horns where they don't belong, Liege Maximo?" he said.

The mischief-maker leaped up in shock, preparing to blast Micronus.

"Let's not bother with a fight," Micronus said, hovering confidently in front of the horned bot. "We both know we're too evenly matched for it to amount to anything but a waste of time."

Liege Maximo's optics flared with anger.

"Time is all we have, Micronus! Don't you see how infinitely boring this realm has become? Manipulating these inconsequential Autobots is my new favourite pastime."

"Well, your 'fun' is done, trickster!" Micronus snapped.

Liege Maximo's horns twitched.

He made a grand gesture with his hands and a smile cracked across his face.

"On the contrary, Micronus. My fun is NOT done ... It has only just begun!"

Back on Earth, Bumblebee pulled himself up from the puddle of oil. Optimus's eerie face wasn't a trick of the light – it was staring up at the Autobot leader with hatred in its optics.

"BUMBLEBEE," the voice echoed through the canyon. "YOU ARE A FOOL TO STAND AGAINST US. YOUR TEAM WILL FALL ONE BY ONE – JUST LIKE THE BOT THAT YOU HAVE ALREADY FAILED."

Skinkbomb, Grimlock, and Strongarm looked around to see the source of the booming voice.

"Sir, why does that voice sound like Optimus?" Strongarm asked, drawing her blaster into a ready-to-fire position.

125

"Whoa," Grimlock said. "Maybe we've *all* got brain rust!"

"No, Grim, this is nothing more than a trick," Bumblebee said. "Is this your doing, Decepticon?"

Skinkbomb had taken advantage of the confusion and scurred back to the oil.

"I'm not responsible for this spooky stereo act, but I sure enjoy dinner and a show!" The Decepticon began shovelling metal scraps and great gulps of oil into his wide mouth.

"You're going on a diet, Skinkbomb!" Bumblebee shouted. "Grimlock, clean his plate for him!"

Grimlock nodded and transformed into his Tyrannosaurus mode. The brutish bot smashed his tail into the ground, creating

a shockwave that sent the remaining oil
cans rolling across the quarry floor.
With another wide swing of his tail,
Grimlock swatted the metal out of
Skinkbomb's claws.

"Strongarm, let's defuse this explosive situation!" Bee said.

The law-bot leaped onto Skinkbomb's back, pinning the Decepticon's arms. Bumblebee dashed over and grabbed hold of the nearly complete tail-bomb.

"GIVE UP, BUMBLEBEE!" the imposter Optimus shouted. "WE DECEPTICONS ARE LEGION. YOU CANNOT DEFEAT US ALL!"

"I might not be able to defeat you all by myself," Bumblebee said, tugging on the tail bomb. "But, luckily, I don't have to!"

Grimlock, back in bot mode, grabbed hold alongside Bumblebee. With Strongarm keeping Skinkbomb's arms bound, Bumblebee and Grimlock succeeded in pulling the criminal's tail bomb loose!

"TOO LATE, AUTOBOT FOOLS!" the voice boomed.

Bumblebee looked at the tail bomb in his hands. It was ticking!

"Autobots, burn rubber!"

Bumblebee threw the bomb over his shoulder, and the three bots rushed away with their captive in tow. They made it to the edge of the quarry before the force from the explosion knocked them flat.

KRAKA-BOOOOOM!

Bumblebee, Grimlock, and Strongarm stumbled to their treads, their audio receptors still ringing.

Skinkbomb tried to scurry into the surrounding forest, but Grimlock grabbed the slippery lizardbot in an iron grip.

"It's going to take more than a cheap imitation of Optimus and a few firecrackers to defeat this team!" Bumblebee said proudly.

In the Realm of the Primes, Optimus waited and meditated.

When his mentor, Micronus, left to confront Liege Maximo, he had warned Optimus to prepare for an attack.

I have learned much during these simulated exercises, Optimus thought to himself. I may need more time and training before I'm prepared to face this impending evil, but I'm ready now for anything Liege Maximo can conjure up!

A fog began to roll across the ground, carrying with it ominous cries from all directions:

"Earth has fallen!"

"Bumblebee betrayed us all!"

"How could the Autobots abandon us like this?"

The red-and-blue Autobot leader climbs to his feet and calmly drew his sword. He spoke evenly into the void, no trace of emotion in his voice.

"Your tricks and taunts don't bother me, Liege Maximo. They never did."

Optimus's optics scanned the fog.

Several figures appeared in the distance,

rapidly making their way towards his position. Then images of Bumblebee, Strongarm, Grimlock, Sideswipe, and Fixit leaped out of the fog and attacked Optimus!

Optimus carved his blade in a wide arc, slashing through his attackers without hesitation.

WHOOSH!

Five of the six false Autobots fell to the ground and shattered into fragments of quickly disappearing light.

SKEESH!

Only the evil Bumblebee remained.

"Your confidence in these bots is misplaced, Optimus," Bumblebee said. "They will let you down. They are weak and easily manipulated!"

"I don't think so, Liege Maximo," Optimus replied. "Bumblebee and the other bots are the bravest, most trustworthy bots I know. The only weak one I see around here is you."

Before the fake Bumblebee could respond, Optimus stepped forward and drove his blade through the illusion, sending it scattering into flickers of light.

FWISSSS!

"Curses! It's not fair! It's not—" an angry voice echoed through the Realm before being abruptly cut off.

When Optimus turned around, Micronus was hovering before him once more.

"You done good, kid," Micronus said.

"Has Liege Maximo been defeated?" Optimus asked.

"It's not as simple as that. Liege Maximo might be a menace, but he is one of us." Micronus said. "The Primes will find a way to punish him, though. I promise you that."

"And his tricks?"

"Over for now," Micronus replied. "And even if he tried again, you and Bumblebee are too wise for him."

"Bumblebee?" Optimus asked. "Did Liege Maximo involve the real Bumblebee in all of this?"

"Oh, yeah, I forgot to mention – Liege Maximo was tinkering with your pal on Earth in the same way. Confused him for a nanocycle or two, but Bumblebee shook it off just like you did. Seems he isn't too shabby of a leader himself."

Optimus beamed with pride. Once again his former lieutenant had done a great job.

"You might want to give him a few words of encouragement, though," Micronus said. "Never hurts to hear a kind word from a friend."

He waved his hands and opens a portal to the scrapyard. Bumblebee and the other bots were gathered around Fixit's repair table.

Sideswipe picked himself up, clutching at his injured back with a grimace.

"Solus knows I could sure use a buff job!" he quipped.

Bumblebee felt a wash of relief that his friend and team-mate was almost back to normal.

"Don't rush your repair phase, Sideswipe," Bumblebee said, gently pushing the younger bot back down to the table. "I think your heroism earned you a few cycles of rest mode."

"What would you do without me, Bee?" Sideswipe asked.

"Let's not answer that," Bumblebee said with a laugh.

With Skinkbomb safely deposited in a stasis pod and Sideswipe looking better, the bots were looking forward to a little peace and quiet.

Suddenly, their brief peace was interrupted by a much-too-familiar voice booming through the audio system.

"BUMBLEBEE!"

"Oh no, not this again!" Bumblebee said.

He pulled his blaster and aimed it at the screen where Optimus's face had materialised.

"This is no trick, Bee," Optimus explained.

Bumblebee cautiously lowered his weapon.

" ... Optimus?"

"I wish I could explain everything to you, but I can't. With time, I will. But what I can tell you is that you're a wise, worthy leader – and a fantastic friend."

"I knew you couldn't be a Decepticon, Optimus," Bumblebee said. "There's no one I trust more on Earth, Cybertron, or wherever you are now."

The other bots looked on with smiles as their leader reconnected with his mentor.

"I'm being tested in the Realm of the Primes, Bumblebee," Optimus stated. "And I think you and I just won an unexpected battle. So, in a way, we were fighting side by side like the good old days. I'm grateful

that Earth is under the watch of a
confident, clear-headed Autobot like you,
Bumblebee. You and your team have
made me proud."

Bumblebee stood tall with his friends
beaming around him.

As quickly as it appeared, the vision of
Optimus began to fade.

"And in some time soon," Optimus
said, "I'll be proud to protect Earth
alongside you once again!"

· · · MISSION COMPLETE · · ·

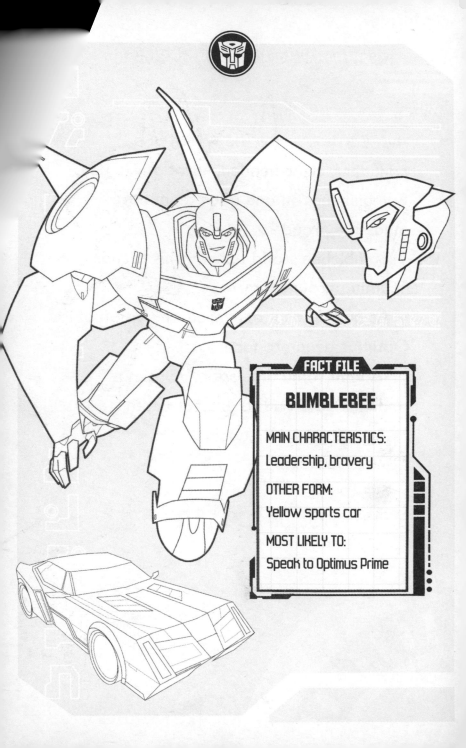

FACT FILE

BUMBLEBEE

MAIN CHARACTERISTICS:
Leadership, bravery

OTHER FORM:
Yellow sports car

MOST LIKELY TO:
Speak to Optimus Prime

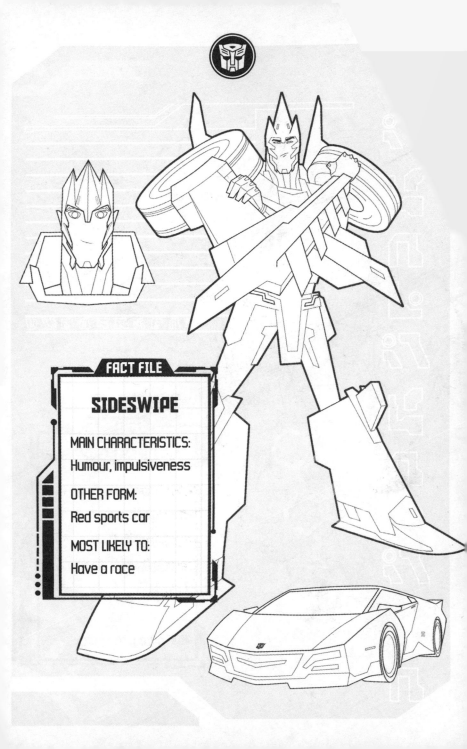

FACT FILE

SIDESWIPE

MAIN CHARACTERISTICS:
Humour, impulsiveness

OTHER FORM:
Red sports car

MOST LIKELY TO:
Have a race

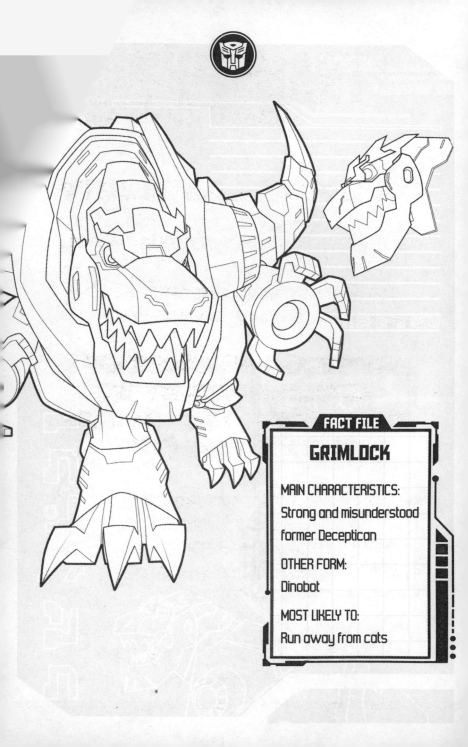

FACT FILE

GRIMLOCK

MAIN CHARACTERISTICS:
Strong and misunderstood
former Deceptican

OTHER FORM:
Dinobot

MOST LIKELY TO:
Run away from cats

CALLING ALL AUTOBOTS

We have a Transformers toy bundle to give away!

If you want to be in with a chance to receive this
awesome prize just answer this question:

WHAT IS THE NAME OF OPTIMUS PRIME'S TEACHER IN THE REALM OF THE PRIMES?

te your answer on the back of a postcard and send it to:
Transformers Competition
Hachette Children's Group
Carmelite House, 50 Victoria Embankment
London, EC4Y 0DZ

Closing Date: December 2nd 2017

For full terms and conditions go to
tps://www.hachettechildrens.co.uk/TermsandConditions/transformerscompetitionoptimus.page